. . . for parents and teachers

How do we instill a sense of discipline in our children regarding their obligations to others? And how can we educate them about the value of these commitments?

Mere prescription or force will never insure the continuation of these behaviors without routine outside influence. In addition to our own guidance and direction, we must be willing to set examples and model appropriate behavior. Only with such support will children begin to develop a sense of responsibility for themselves.

Besides examples and encouragement, we can also expose children to responsibility through activities and through literature. *Do I Have To?* describes self-centered, selfish behavior — and more responsible behavior. It does so in ways that a child can easily understand, thereby recognizing the advantages of "responsible" social behavior.

I have read this story to young children, and have found it an excellent stimulus to discussion. In fact, I was pleasantly surprised by the enthusiastic responses. Be prepared for a torrent of opinions.

MANUEL S. SILVERMAN, Ph.D.
ASSOCIATE PROFESSOR AND CHAIR
DEPARTMENT OF GUIDANCE AND
    COUNSELING
LOYOLA UNIVERSITY OF CHICAGO

Copyright © 1980, Raintree Publishers Inc.

Library of Congress Number: 79-23890

  10 11 12 13 14 99 98 97 96 95 94

Printed in the United States of America.

Library of Congress Cataloging in Publication Data

Quigley, Stacy.
  Do I have to?

  SUMMARY: Ruben complains about having to write thank-
you letters, return borrowed items, and admit his mistakes
until he sees the advantages of less selfish behavior.
  [1. Selfishness — Fiction] I. Lexa, Susan. II. Title.
PZ7.Q416Do   [Fic]   79-23890
ISBN 0-8172-1352-X Hardcover Library Binding
ISBN 0-8114-2536-3 Softcover Binding

DO I HAVE TO?

by Stacy Quigley

illustrated by Susan Lexa

introduction by Manuel S. Silverman, Ph.D.

RSVP

RAINTREE STECK-VAUGHN
P U B L I S H E R S
The Steck-Vaughn Company

Austin, Texas

"Ruben!" called his mother. "Hurry up! You got a package in the mail today."

Ruben tumbled down the stairs. "What is it?" he asked.

"Open it and see. I think it's from Aunt Harriet."

Ruben tore away the paper and opened the box.

"Oh, boy!" he shouted. "A space helmet!"

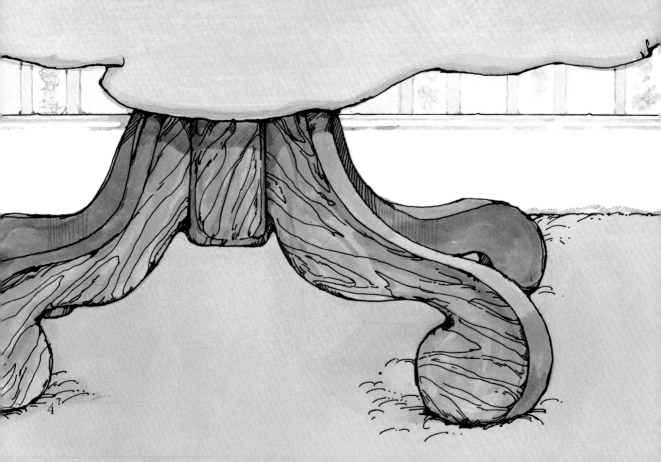

5

His mother smiled. "You'll have to write Aunt Harriet right away and thank her."

"Do I have to?" Ruben groaned. "I hate writing letters."

"I know, but when someone sends you a present, you should say thank you."

"Can I do it later?" Ruben asked. "I want to show my friends the helmet."

"All right, but don't forget."

Ruben didn't mean to, but he *did* forget to write the thank-you letter. There was always something more important to do, like play ball, watch TV, or do homework.

Weeks went by.

One day Ruben received a letter:

Dear Ruben,
  Did you ever get my
  package? I think it got
  lost in the mail. Please
  let me know.
    Love, Aunt Harriet

"Uh-oh," Ruben said to himself. "I guess I'd better write now. Wait — I have a better idea. Maybe I can draw a picture instead. That's more fun."

Dear Ritben,
Did you ever ~ think
my package? I think
it got lost in the
mail. Please let
me know. Love,
Aunt Hanna.

11

He rushed into his sister's room.
"Sandy, can I borrow your crayons?"
"Forget it," said Sandy.
"What do you mean?"
"I let you take my crayons once before,
and I never saw them again. Go get your
own."

13

Ruben tried his father. "Dad, could I have some money for crayons?"

"Didn't we just buy you some crayons a little while ago?"

"Oh, I lost those. Sandy has some, but she won't lend them to me."

"Why?" asked Ruben's father.

"I don't know. I guess I forgot to return the ones I borrowed from her before."

"I'll tell you what," his father said. "I think you should earn the money and buy them yourself."

"Do I have to?" asked Ruben. "Couldn't you just —"

"And I know just where you can earn the money," his father went on. "Ms. Fraser down the street needs someone to cut her lawn. She'll pay you enough for the crayons."

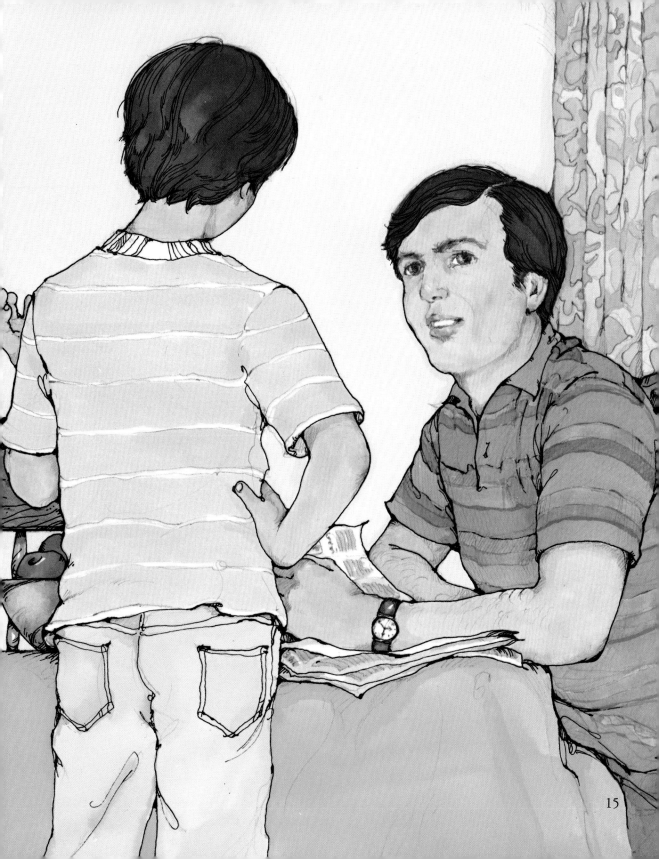

Later that day, Ms. Fraser showed
Ruben where her lawn mower was.

"Be careful," she told him. "I like my
yard to look neat."

The lawn mower was old and heavy.
Ruben had to push hard to get it going,
and he had to pull hard to make it stop.

Just as Ruben was about to finish the
lawn, the mower slipped out of his hands.

Crash! It rolled straight into a rosebush. Branches snapped. Flowers scattered. Ruben tried to pick up as much of the bush as he could. Then he hurried to put the mower away.

19

Ms. Fraser stepped out onto her porch. "Are you all done?" she called.

"Er, yes, I am," said Ruben, his face red.

"Good. I'll go get you a cold drink and your pay."

Before she went inside, Ms. Fraser took a look around her yard.

"My roses!" she screeched. "What happened?"

Ruben's face turned redder. "I'm really sorry. I couldn't stop the mower. . . ."

"Weren't you even going to tell me what happened?"

"I was sort of hoping you wouldn't notice. . . ."

"Not notice!" she said. "You'd better go home. It's bad enough that you ruined my flowers. But trying to hide it was worse."

Ruben slowly walked home.

"How did the job go?" asked Ruben's father.

"Terrible." Ruben explained what had happened. "I just can't do anything right."

"That's not true," said his father. He dipped a brush into a can and began painting the fence. "You just found out that it's better to be honest about your mistakes."

"But it's not fair!" Ruben exploded. "I always have to do things I don't want to do. I have to write letters, give back crayons, tell people my mistakes. . . . Why do I have to do all that stuff?"

"We all have to do things we don't like."

"But why?"

"It's just good manners," said Ruben's father. "Good manners mean thinking of others, not just yourself all the time. Sometimes that takes extra work. But in the long run, manners make life easier."

Ruben watched his father paint for a while. "Well, I still don't have the money for the crayons," he said finally.

His father stood up and pulled their lawn mower out into the yard.
"Want to try again — this time with our lawn?"
"Sure!"

Later that week, Ruben received a phone call from Aunt Harriet.

"I just loved your drawing," she said. "I got it today, and I already taped it to my wall."

"Can you tell what it is?" asked Ruben. "It's a picture of me in a rocket. I'm wearing the helmet."

"Of course I can tell. You're a very good artist," she said.

"Thanks!"

To himself, Ruben thought, *Maybe Dad was right about this manners stuff, after all.*

27

After the phone call, Ruben went to Sandy's room.

"Do you want to shoot some baskets?" Sandy asked.

"Later. We promised to help Mom clean the basement, don't you remember?"

Sandy gave him a funny look. "Playing basketball is more fun than cleaning," she said as she followed him down to the basement.

"I know. But we shouldn't break a promise. That's bad manners."

"Since when did you learn so much about manners?" Sandy laughed.

"Learning manners is like learning to ride a bike," answered Ruben. "After a while you don't think about it. You just do it."

"Well, I don't know whether to believe you or not. I think you're just afraid that I'm going to be better at shooting baskets than you are!"

Ruben smiled. "We'll just see about *that* after we get through with the basement," he said. "And that's a promise!"

31